God's Fr

Do You Glance or Gaze Into Your Daily Mirror?

Elrich Martin

Published by Revival Waves of Glory Books & Publishing

PO Box 596 | Litchfield, Illinois 62056 USA

www.revivalwavesofgloryministries.com

Revival Waves of Glory Books & Publishing is committed to excellence in the publishing industry.

Book design Copyright © 2016 by Revival Waves of Glory Books & Publishing. All rights reserved.

Published in the United States of America

Paperback: 978-1-68411-039-1

Table of contents

Introduction

Please allow me to introduce my new book with two stories of endearment for the two main characters, Enrico and Alison who go through a journey of discovery and contentment in facing their different obstacles in life and to learning to withstand their different tests. There are a mixture of joy, heartache, discovery of self and suspense all leading to the same purpose for both individuals. If you believe in the supernatural then this is for you. This is a book for those who wonder why it feels as if they are always at the wrong end of life and what they can use to be content and be victorious in their life. These stories will have you live these pages as you read them, some might see their own lives play like a movie as they read, feeling themselves within these pages as they become one with the characters of this book.

Dedication

I want to dedicate this book of all to the Alpha and Omega, Lord Father God Jesus Christ for giving me the grace and wisdom to write the details for this story. I would not have been able to pour my vision into these words without God. I also want to thank the Holy Spirit for lying thoughts and visions within my heart during this time of revelation. It is such an honor to feel the presence of the Holy Spirit when you are writing, when I didn't know what to add on text, there was always a thought given to me through grace. I also want to dedicate this book to my wife, Mrs. Shamelle Martin for her support and help with proofreading this book. She told me she loved this book on a neutral level as I asked and she gave me her upbeats opinion and she gave me the inspiration to finish this work. Lastly, I want to thank my two daughters, Gabriella and Zoe for their presence in my life and for giving me the strength to pursue my vision with my wife. I love you dearly. I dedicate this book also to all to readers that will enter these pages. I hope you will find joy in this word and a comfort in your heart.

Foreword

Genesis 1;27 reads as follows, So God created mankind in his own image, in the image of God he created them, male and female he created them. So we were basically created the same, so we have been created as mere mirrors of each other. We are all mirrors to each other every day in our daily life. What do you see each morning when you look in the mirror? Do you see yourself as Gods image or your own self-image where the outer matter more than the inner? Do you realize you and me are representing God on this earth and it is such an honor but the devil whom was an angel once and wanted to be God, is so jealous of us as God have created us in his image and not him that he uses individuals everyday as puppets, hiding behind their mirrors in school, at the office, in church, in government, you name it, he will be there. He reflects his negativity through us as human mirrors to infect others with his sins he wants to reflect on us all. He is merely shifting a mirror of negativity, anger, hate etc. and positioning that mirror towards a mirror of positiveness to create a reflection which would change the positive to the negative. Making and example, if someone, a total stranger, looks at you with disgust, anger and hate, most of us may also change our facial expression to mimic their actions but the solution is to overcome the negative expression with a positive reaction. Showing a smile to a frowning face is hard to do, I know but it will break the devils strangle hold and it will have an effect for the better. Stay strong though your daily encounter of mirrors. Not all mirrors have a bad reflection and we have the power to change the devils image to a heavenly reflection.

God's faith mirror

Do you glance or gaze into your daily mirror?

Every day in our lives, we are affected by mirrors. Not the ones we use to admire ourselves in and see the outer self. I'm referring to the inner mirrors of everyday life. We cross paths with them in our house, when we leave our house, in the car, in traffic, on the way to work, within the workplace etc.. These mirrors have a different effect on us every day we view them. Some make us sad, others make us happy. From the moment you are born, your mirror had an effect on your parents, family, friends and even strangers. Mostly the mirror reflects happiness at that time of your life. Even though you as a baby cannot grasp the affect your mirror had on those around you, its will become reality once you grow into your toddler years when you start to realize the mirrors surrounding you is causing your emotions to fluctuate. From happiness to crying from joy to sadness. Your little mind at that time cannot comprehend the reality of the daily mirrors as most as your mirrors at that time on your life are clean, without secrets, anger, depression, financial stress and all that comes with it. Your mirror is without blemish nor guilt, nor shame. We all know what our mirrors are hiding; some reflect the hurt and pain on others, even more, when the crack in our mirror have not healed. Our constant effort to fulfill what we see in others on ourselves can have a positive or negative effect. The youth sees the adaptive culture of pants being pulled down when walking as a sign on coolness and the mirror they see in most cases are the mirror they want to reflect upon themselves. Why is it that some of the youth will use that mirror and reflect it on themselves and some won't? Could it be that they wanted to be like the person or be the person or trying to escape their current reflection of how they see themselves? The mirror you reflect for others to see can only be changed by you and if you give God the opportunity to clean your reflection so you can see what others see in you. This is a story of reflections of a child in his environment and the choices he made to change the way his mirror reflect on others during his life. Enrico and Alison are two individuals from different walks of lives but with one spiritual purpose, to find their purpose and find Gods purpose for them.

ENRICO'S STORY

Chapter 1:

The Mirror of Happiness

Enrico was 6 years old, first day of school. Boy, he was so afraid but his grandma took him to school. He had a mother but she could not take care of him. To him, his grandma was his reflection of a mother and she was his everything. First day school was a testing phase, having a name board around his neck so he can be identified by name and the teacher talking a lot of foreign things not yet sunk in. He just wanted to play, carefree. He befriended some boys because at that age you don't judge nor look at the outer, you see a friend that you can play cars with or whatever comes up. Hi, said Enrico to the other boy, what is your name. The other boy did not give his name but did play with him. An innocent mind does not take any offence and they played joyfully. The day finished at school and grandma came to fetch him. Grandma asked Enrico, so how was your day? It was fine, Enrico replied. The term fine at that age really means fine. As one grows older the meaning can differ from the feeling. The school days would go on, day by day and the Enrico noticed that most of his friends at school were brought to school by their parents, a father and a mother. He at that point was thinking where his father was, though he knew his mother outwardly, she was more a mirror of a stranger than a reflection of a mother. He thought of his grandma as his mother and as long as he saw her, he was happy. At that stage of his life, he was not aware that so many children are not so fortunate to have a grandma or grandpa as he had and mostly their mirror reflects no one, only a foster home. He was just so happy as he grandma raised him like her own. His grandpa also raised him like his own. Tin Tin!, his grandpa would call him, his nickname, named after a cartoon character. Grandpa worked at a paper factory and sometimes he would bring Enrico old cartoon books they threw away. He would wait patiently for grandpa to come home, waiting for that book with excitement. He did not always get a book, but he was just happy he could see his grandpa. Their reflections on him as parents had a great effect on himself as the years passed on.

Chapter 2:
The Mirror of Envy

Enrico, now 12 years old is discovering new things that at that age matters, brand toys, clothes and shoes. At school, he was one of a few children who did not wear the brand shoes and clothes talked about in that era. He knew his grandparents would not be able to afford to buy him what he wanted but what was needed, food was provided for. He was not ungrateful but longed in his heart to afford the wants that he sees. Thinking daily, why do we not have what others have? Why am I being made fun of at school because of my torn clothes and shoes? Enrico at that time wished he had a magic lamp, where he could summon a genie to grant him his three want wishes because the brand mirrors were what he wanted. Didn't we all at some point of our lives envied someone for what they have and who they are? Well, it is one of life's lessons that we learn that the reelections of riches are not the need of the heart but the wants of the mind. Enrico grew up in a poor neighborhood where the mirrors of poverty have been viewed and reflected from generation to generation, carried over by the same vision. He wanted to become a famous cricket star one day and provide for his grandma and grandpa who have given so much to him. Even though there was a lack of material things, there was love and feeling of belonging to his grandparents. Enrico felt so loved but he had to learn a lesson in life, that the natural does not last forever. The reflections of current reality in our lives are not to be carried over. Your mirror is not permanent, be of good cheer as the mirror vision will be changed by God if you do not get swept in by the vision of your current situation.

Chapter 3:
The Mirror of Loss

At 14, Enrico was going to high school. Not what he was looking forward to as he was quite shy. He was always being pestered by the girls and he did not want it, though liking the attention, he wanted to focus on his studies and provide for his grandparents. His grandfather had asthma and it started to get worse. Grandpa used to say tin, tin are you ok and then would wipe my face after he washed his hands and inserted his false teeth, which I did not like but it was funny though. Grandpa started to get more and more asthma attacks. It was heartbreaking for Enrico and his grandma to see him, so helpless. He can remember seeing his grandpa for the last time in his bedroom, looking at him, looking tired of the suffering, struggling for air, tears in his eyes looking at Enrico with a father's eye. Even in struggle he could feel grandpa's love for him. The ambulance came and took him away. Later that night they got an opportunity to go see grandpa. At his hospital bed, grandpa looked at grandma and said, I'm so grateful to have had a wife like you sweetie, that was his nickname for her. Enrico could feel his grandma's pain. His grandpa kept praising grandma and he said a prayer but his grandpa's eyes were different, a haziness over them. Death was near. They stayed there for a while but had to leave. He greeted and his grandfather's last words to him were, bye tin, tin. They received a call later that night that grandpa passed away. For Enrico it was like losing a father, a role model. Why did this happen? Why did God take him? Why is nothing working out? Reality filled his mind that if his grandpa died then his grandma will also soon die and he could not deal with losing both. In the lowest point of his life, he decided to take his own life. If I die before my grandma then he won't feel this pain again, Enrico thought and swallowed a handful of grandpa's asthma and blood pressure pills but afterwards were sick and were taken to hospital but would be survived?

Chapter 4:
The Mirror of Acceptance

The pills he took made him vomit a lot and he was given a bed while they pumped his stomach. During that night, Enrico was lying on his side, alone in the hospital room trying to figure out what happened and why he did what he did. Things would never be the same. The emptiness felt by this grandfather's absence were too hard to swallow. At our lowest point in our lives, we tend to reflect on negative mirrors surrounding us, as death is a representation of a shattered mirror which in the natural cannot be fixed even by the most skilled artisan. The wants in the mirror at that point cannot comprehend for the loss so hurtful. Therefore we need to view our Lord father God, Jesus Christ, who is our perfect mirror, free from loss, free from envy, free from pain and focus on the spiritual mirror of our God as a reflection of our imperfections, forgiven by the one who have no sins. Enrico did not yet know what he had in him, his spiritual mirror. Therefore he were spared from death as his purpose on earth, his spiritual mirror is not at its end yet and he will learn as time go on, the purpose that all these mirrors had in his life. He had to accept the mirror of love and acceptance that reflected in his grandfather's mirror were passed on to him and the memories will never be forgotten but they will one day be together again in the heavenly mirror.

Chapter 5:
Bible Verses Regarding Mirrors

Let's reflect on bible verses where mirrors are the topic as quoted in the holy bible

1 Corinthians 13:12 (new international version) For now we see only a reflection as in a mirror, then we shall see face to face. Now I know in part, then I shall know fully, even as I am fully known.

2 Corinthians 3:18 (new American standard bible) But we all, with unveiled face, beholding as in a mirror the glory of the Lord, are being transformed into the same image from glory to glory, just as from the Lord, the spirit.

James 1:23 (new international version) Anyone who listens to the word but does not do what it says is like a someone who looks at his face in the mirror

Proverbs 27:19-21 Just as water mirrors your face, so your face mirrors your heart

Genesis 1:27 So God created mankind in his own image, in the image of God he created them, male and female he created them

God's word is a mirror. It's the same as a natural mirror that you look in to see what you need to change or leave as is before you start the day. The mirror is an image of what you were and what you are and what you can be. You can choose how your life story goes, by grasping on the word of God and reflecting God's word to the world. Enrico made mistakes in his weakness, but we all have to change something, sometimes as our image isn't always as seeing our reflection, but once we learn to change into the correct spiritual attire, we will see ourselves as God sees us.

Chapter 6:
The Mirror of Discovery

After the loss of Enrico's grandfather, things were tighter financially .The breadwinner and father have left for heaven and sleeping hungry became a normal occurrence. Enrico was being taunted at school because he did not wear the in style shoes and he did not want to be part of the gangster activities which were labeled as cool. He just wanted to finish his school so he can provide for his grandmother. Seeing her suffer to keep head above water was a nail in his heart. Dreaming of giving his pooki, her other nickname given by her husband a better life was his main motivation. She always held her head high, even in tough circumstances, a mother of worth. A woman who took her daughter's son as her own, without judging and took the role as if she gave birth to Enrico. Enrico realized that he could do all through prayer as that was the way he was brought up, to honor God. He can remember his grandfather putting him in the front basket of his bicycle and rode to church even when he wanted to play. When you realize your potential, you see the future and visualize you achieving through belief. Enrico was determined to succeed as he saw an image in his mind of the smile on his grandmama's face, free of worry and proud of her son. He was now the man of the house and he was determined to give her the life she deserves. So our Lord also wants the best for us, more than we can imagine. Enrico did not know how his life would turn out as he still had the mirror of his community and family and how one generation have followed the same of the previous one. Where the whole family of uncles, aunts, sisters, brothers have worked at the same factory for minimal wage, lived in their house of birth their whole life and did not see a future beyond what was reflected from the family mirrors. God want the best for us and want us to step out of the boat of our current situation to new heights. All we need to do is to change the way we look at ourselves and declare the favor of God is with us. Enrico told his grandma while they were sitting in the living room, Mommy, I'm going to make something of my life and take you out of here. Mommy just smiled proudly and said, yes Enrico you will. She reflected faith on his life and that made him so grateful for her presence.

Chapter 7:

The Mirror of Disappointment

At school, things got worse for Enrico. Being called names for trying to just do what's right and learn was a daily routine. The children admired the mirror of gangsters' and the false reflection of coolness and money it brings. They would come to school with their cars and were almost idolized. Enrico asked a girl one day what she thought of the gangsterism? She told him she would to anything to be like them and she think they are so cool. For Enrico, this was a place he did not want to be in. His grandma could not afford to send him to a proper school where he could learn without being harassed and he decided in desperation to do something he never thought he would do. At 16 Enrico was tired of all the rejections and loss he had. Why does everyone hate me? What did I do wrong? Even my own parents did not want me. Depression started to kick in. The mirror he saw at school was one he wanted to break. He planned one day not to go to school and took a blade and cut himself to make as if he was attacked. He went home and saw the hurt in his grandma's eyes at seeing him hurt. As he looked at his grandma, he said without talking, I'm sorry mommy that I'm lying to you but the pain I inflicted with this cut is nothing compared to the pain I had to endure day in and day out, please forgive me, mommy! He could not say that to her and it hurt him so much to keep this secret but he had to get out. Enrico left school but his grandma but his grandma enrolled him at a learn from home study program where he would study at home and then write grade 12 exams at a college nearby. He did grade 12 and passed that same year. He was grade 10 the same year at the other school. His grandma was so proud, he secretly saw her write on a card, putting it in an envelope and putting in the mailbox. Then she called Enrico to see if there were any mail and, surprise that were priceless. Disappointment turned into happiness, something good happened at last, he thought.

Chapter 8:
Understanding the Effect of the Spiritual Mirror

Before we go further, let's look at the definition of a mirror which is, something that shows what another thing is like in a very clear and accurate way. That is how God see us, in a clear and perfect way. We tend to want to change the mirror, but the mirror can't change its reflection unless we change ourselves and see our reflection as God see us. The bible is the best mirror we can read to reflect on. The bible is unlike any mirror because it can actually change us. God see us so differently than how we see ourselves. In the morning, when you look in the mirror what do you see, wrinkles, uncombed hair, pimples. Well spiritually that is how some people see themselves, full of sin, they cannot be forgiven for what they have done. We'll see yourself how God see you, righteous. You are the righteousness of God in Christ. Nothing that hides from others are hidden from God. Nothing you have done secretly or openly cannot be forgiven. You need to confess and receive the forgiveness that was freely given to us all two thousand years ago. If your mirror is made unclear due to your thoughts about yourself, how can others then take in your reflection? Do not let your past determine your future. You are Gods child and he wants to take your hand and wipe you clean of all your mistakes and let you shine, through grace.

Chapter 9:
The Mirror of Faith in Pain

Enrico, now 24, have been in and out of jobs, not getting a permanent position and finally things were starting to look up when he received a job offer and he took it. It was a position with health insurance and a steady contract, renewable. He was so happy that he told his grandma and he started to think about getting them a place in a better area and getting mommy health insurance. Her health started to deteriorate during this period. He would walk with her slowly where she would collect her pension, she made sure she dressed for the occasion every pension day and she would tell me, Enrico ,my feet feels as if they are on fire. He would then tell her, don't worry, he will get him health insurance and she can get the best care. Mommy did not get better, she started to get unbearable pain in her legs, they later found out she had gangrene due to the diabetes. It was a testing time for both Enrico and his grandma. One night she screamed so much of the pain, she could not bear it anymore and they got someone to take her to hospital. Once in her hospital bed, morphine in her body to take away this nasty pain, he could sense her relief. Enrico would visit her every day at hospital as he was due to start work at following month and he would spend time with his spiritual mother at her bedside, make jokes, listen to her complain softly about the staff and just let her express herself. While she is talking, he looked at her and he saw the same mommy as the one who used to iron his clothes he wanted, made his tea, waited for him to get home at night, kept his food warm for him every time he came home and never complained. I wish I would see her so pain-free forever, he thought. She was discharged from hospital and she got worse again, heart attacks followed, hospital in, hospital out. She could not walk without assistance anymore and Enrico had to lead her to the bathroom and back. She felt so ashamed at her dependence on him but for Enrico, this was nothing compared to what she did for him. For what is a mother worth other than priceless? Enrico learned how to make food and iron his clothes as his mommy could no longer do what she could before. New Year's Day came and he and his uncle made food. Mommy requested them to make a Cornish hen, something she ate as a child which they did the best they could. That day, mommy looked much better, were laughing and eating cheese and crackers behind Enrico's back as he did not want her to eat dairy due to her diabetes but he was just happy that she was happy. The day after New Year's Day, Enrico took his then girlfriend to the station as she had to go home but he received a message along the way that his grandma is ill again. He rushed home and found her in a terrible state. No, this can't be happening he thought, she collapsed and hit her head against the toilet bowl. As if in a nightmare, Enrico yelled MOMMY, MOMMY! He lifted her up and put her on the bed and ambulance came and he went with to hospital. Sitting in the ambulance with his mommy, still trying to figure out what happened; his grandmother looked at him and said she is thirsty. Mommy, I will get water for you now by the hospital, we are almost there. That were her last words to him and her spirit was transferred to heaven. At hospital, they tried everything to revive her but it was too late. Seeing her lifeless body, eyes half open was like he was slowly dying of heartache. His uncle came and managed to get him away from his mommy's body and in the parking area Enrico, not being able to handle to reality of it all, fell down and cried because his mirror is gone.

Chapter 10:

Reflections on Life After Death

Enrico lost a part of himself that day at hospital. A part lost that he never thought can ever be replaced. Have you ever lost a mirror? A reflection of love and affection lost in an instant? Enrico was confused and blamed himself for not helping his mommy, not being able to afford to provide the health care she needed. He walked to a railway track nearby and sat with a few homeless people there. He shared with them a bottle of vodka he had bought sleeping pills to enter the place his grandmother went to and to leave this earth full of disappointment and pain. He lost his purpose and told them what happened. Sorry to hear about what happened, one of them said. Enrico was too angry, more fueled by the vodka to understand the helping hand of others behind him. Enrico was about to swallow the pills when one the guys took the pills from him saying, this is not the way to go. Enrico was too angry and left. Why did God take her away! Why does he hate me! What did I do to deserve this!

This was all the questions Enrico had. He fainted and the next thing he knew he was in hospital with alcohol intoxication. Why didn't he just die he thought? That night while in hospital, alone in his room, lying on his side, he felt his grandma sitting at the back of him but he could not turn over to see her. She told him she does not want him to take drugs and alcohol and as if she were still alive, they had a conversation even though he could not see her. He went to sleep and woke up and every time he felt the presence of family members by his bed as if God sent angels through the night to guard over him. He could remember a vision of his grandmother and she looked concerned about him. The whole night, Enrico could not recall ever being alone. He believed God sent his angels to reflect their mirrors on him as he had lost his mirror in the natural and needed the spiritual mirror of understanding and faith. The next day Enrico were discharged from hospital, but even though the pain of losing his mommy was still there, he had a sense that she was happy where she was at peace and she wanted the best for him and so did God. He was reminded by God in a dream later that night where his grandma told him she was dead now she is alive and she looked very happy. That was the spiritual mirror providing Enrico with hope that he will survive and all is not lost. Enrico started to think of loving memories he had of his grandma and what she meant to him. Her words in the spirit touched him and he dedicated his life's purpose to God and the spiritual mirror that he received.

Chapter 11:
Mirrors of the Meaning of Faith

Enrico decided to go to church but he was skeptical. Was he ready to give his life over to the lord? The mirror of doubt reflected on a time in life before when he went to a church conference and there was a request for those seeking work to come forward. Enrico desperate for a job went forward and then, suddenly the man that prayed for him told everyone, this young man is now saved! Huh, how, what, Enrico could not understand. He wanted to get a job, not ready to be saved yet. The man saw his last cigarette in his shirt pocket took it out and broke it in front of him. Enrico didn't know at that point, if he should laugh or cry or run out of there. His last cigarette mirror of addiction started when he was young, he saw his family members smoke and once, when he was told to kill one of the cigarettes smoked, he secretly took a drag and nearly coughed his lungs out and now he have to make a choice between accepting God and cigarettes. He left that church service with a smoke, yes he found one thinking tomorrow I'll quit but that as expected did not happen. He loved God but the spirit of addiction to nicotine clouded his judgment. He then thought, the God that he knows will accept him even though he smokes. Later in his life he gave his life to Jesus and even though he did not stop immediately, he did stop. Sometimes in our lives we have mirrors of anger, abuse, pain that we experience as a child that we later on reflect on our loved ones because we have not cleaned the mirror, we are still looking in a mirror that hasn't been cleaned for ten, twenty, fifty years, even longer. When you look in the mirror today before you leave your house, the image you saw will not be exactly the same as you will see tomorrow in the same mirror. Do not look in a mirror of today and expect to always see the image of yesterday. The mirror will remain the same, you won't. Enrico lost the faith in himself but regained faith through viewing his girlfriend's mirror. A mirror of belief in him, hope and a future. They started to read the bible together and started to understand what the calling of God has for their lives. He could not understand when his girlfriend told him that she prayed to God to send her someone like him. Does someone like him? He thought. He chuckled as he thought she made a joke but God positioned her mirror of faith to cover his mirror of doubt and gave him hope. He started to remember lying next to his grandma while she screamed in pain and asking God to take her pain away. He realized God did answer his prayer. He gave her everlasting life and took her pain away. He remembered when his grandma was in hospital once for an operation; he stayed at the hospital for the night and was trying to sleep on one of the wooden benches of the pharmacy side of hospital near the elevators. At around 12pm at night, he heard one of the elevators opening and closing. Thinking nothing of it he tried to sleep again then suddenly the other elevators doors opened halfway but did not close. He saw a reflection within the elevator but he could not see what it was so he had to move closer, but he had this weird feeling. When he got close, suddenly this demon face looked at him from the elevator, looking at him with anger. Enrico froze still looking at it and not knowing what will happen. She regained freedom of legs and will all he had, he ran away, looked back while he ran and realized the elevator have closed. He was so thankful to God and yet so scared but felt calm afterwards. Yes, the devil will use his reflection to scare you but he is just a reflection of no power. God's hand of grace was on Enrico that night. Another memory he had was when his grandma was taken into hospital as well and he sat in the waiting room. After 12pm the plants and window blinds started to shake and he was alone. The windows were not open. He was so scared but he kept saying psalm 23 over and over. Then everything stopped and a nurse dressed all white told him to come to his grandmother's room and she showed him a bed to sleep on next to his grandma's bed. The mirror of fear that the devil thought he could use against Enrico was overshadowed by the spiritual mirror of faith of our Lord Jesus. The question Enrico had was how did the nurse know he was there and how did she know he was her grandson. Well, he never saw her again but he believes it was an angel sent to watch over him.

Chapter 12:

Mirror of Understanding and Acceptance of Jesus as Our Savior

Enrico started to understand everything he went through was not permanent. Therefore each mirror he looked at was passing on and new mirrors were approaching of hope and a new life in Christ. He can remember so many happy mirrors through his life and even though his mirrors did not always reflect clearly, he knew God was there to wipe his reflection clean and spotless through accepting Jesus, all past mirrors are removed and new mirrors are due for each phase of his live. The realization is that we meet mirrors with their own reflection every day from all walks of life. Do not trade your mirror of peace for a mirror of turmoil, of joy for stress or faith for unbeliever, the list goes on. There may be people in your path that want you to carry their mirror of negativity as they see your mirror and envy the reflection. Guard your heart against evil as the heart is like a mirror and the spirit the reflection of the mirror.

If you have ever been in a situation where someone is constantly watching you for no reason at all, be at peace that the reflection of your mirror shines through and your mirror of hope, joy, humbleness can be an attraction to those who seek a spiritual mirror. Pray for them and as Enrico, they will have their mirrors cleaned by our Lord Jesus. All he wants is for you to accept him as your Savior.

Enrico found a steady job and have married his girlfriend that shone her mirror on him through God in his dark times. They have two children and very happy. Don't ever think your mirror is too dirty, don't ever think your light cannot have an effect on someone else's mirrors because in the end, we are all mirrors and we reflect on each other, the question is which reflection do you look at in the mirror. Do you look at the mirror of instant fame and fortune or of grace to fulfill your destiny? Do you glance or admire the mirror which is not your destiny.

There are so many Enrico's in the world that have chosen the right mirrors as a path to peace, faith and a living, breathing God. Enrico looked at some mirrors, admired some mirrors and glanced at some, but looked at the spiritual mirror of peace and grace that gave him the best reflection of all.

ALISON'S STORY

Chapter 1:
The Mirror of Neglect

Alison was born in a middle-class family, though she always received the material things she wanted, even when she was a toddler, she was dressed in designer clothes, the best of all. Her father was a sales rep, very busy, almost never at home. He worked seven days a week, mostly away and he was the sole breadwinner. Her mother was a housewife, content with the fact that her husband provided for them, though the gain of the material worth outweighed the intimate that she craved. A man that are there when she need a screw driver to be used to fix a cupboard and not a handyman and a man to hold her when she wants to talk and not an empty house with the material and no love. Well someday it will get better, she thought as he left one more time on his sales rep trips but it became too much for her. Alison, 13 at the time have grown used to her dad not being there, though she missed him at least she could fill his gap with the money and stuff, but is it really so easy? At school, she was popular because she had what she had but when there is a function at school and she sees both parents supporting their children, she felt a pain in her heart. Mom was there sometimes but it just wasn't enough. She never really knew her father. He never came to watch her softball games even when he was home which was seldom as he was too tired then. Alison is getting ready for her softball game and her friend, Jane says: Alison, guess what? What, Alison replied? My parents are here. Yay! Alison sort off gestured. That is the one thing she hated to hear more than anything. Thinking by herself, one day, I will be a good parent to my children, I will come to their games, I will support them. Walking out to the softball pitch, she saw that all her teammates' parents were there, both. Even Jimmy's parents who work nightshift, sacrificed their sleep to come. Alison started to burst out in tears and ran as she could not handle the loneliness. She did not play that day and went home. Her mom is at home, watching television. Why are you home so late, her mom said? Alison just looked at her mom and went to her room. Then her mom remembered, Oh my word, Alison's game was today, I completely forgot. The mirror of neglect was evident on Alison's face and regret was on her mom's fade-In sorry Alison, she said but the house was empty though there were two individuals, there was an emptiness that could not be filled. Alison yearned for the affection of a father and mother that will give her what cannot be found in personal possessions. Sometimes we tend to choose to look at the mirror which were not intended for use for personal growth and then mimic that reflection based on our own wants. Mostly our upbringing from childhood will determine that mirror we choose to invasion our lives on. How come if you look at society, most children with good family values go and do not value the ideals their parents wanted for them. In Alison's case, her parents were both poor growing up and somehow during their lives, the mirror of self-provision were captured by them in their daily reflections through their struggle. They came to the conclusions that a happy child is a child that do not lack materially but they neglected the emotional factor which is key to a happy household where children see and interact with their parents more than the American express card is used as a tool to console which cannot be bought. How will this early mirror in her teens affect Alison and what which mirrors will she choose to capture for her own life?

Chapter 2:
Mirror of Anger

Alison, now 15 have been looking at her family mirror for too long. The lack of interaction between husband and wife and child has taken its toll. Their lives have drifted further and further apart and have come to a point where Alison do not speak to her parents as the title should be but the mirror of anger fueled by the reflections of other families, spoken by her friends at school have taken its toll and the reflection of disrespect have risen. Alison! Her father called but no reply from her. Her father was lying on his bed, tired as can be, just back from a sales call that lasted the entire weekend. Alison? Still no reply. He decided to go to her room and found her there laying and listening to music. Alison! What! She replied. Don't you what me young lady, where is your mother? Alison looked at his with disgust and just said, look on the fridge door. Too tired to argue, her father walked to the fridge. On the way he was thinking, why is my food not ready? Normally she would have my food prepared and warm? Why am I being punished like this by my wife? Why do I even bother? Tiredness, hunger and frustration crept up to him and reality struck when he went to the fridge door and he read the note which read. Dear Kelvin, I have been by your side for 17 years, I have cooked, cleaned and looked after you and Alison but I have not been a part of this family for some time. I love you but we barely know each other anymore, you forgot my birthday for the last 9 years, you have not even text me nor let me know what your sales calls are like, nor have you even remembered your daughter's birthday which was yesterday and you have not once held me for the last three years. Yes I can remember all the stats, because it hurt like hell every time I went through that painful moments in my life and I have decided to go to my sisters to think about what I want to do with my life. Please don't try to contact or come to me, let me figure out the next step. By the way, today is our anniversary, take care. Kelvin still trying to digest all he have read and what is happening. He went to sit down, legs too weak from shock, he could not stand up. The guilt of what he has become has dawned on him and he realized he was on auto-pilot for the past 15 years of their marriage, striving for the mirror of riches and provision of the wants has cost him his family. What have I done, he murmured, holding his head. He started to tremble as he was trying to stand up; he could feel his legs give away from underneath, Alison! Is all he could shout with his best effort as his body crashed onto the floor, he unable to speak further, he so in control or so he thought most of his life are looking from ground level, not knowing what just happened. Alison came walking slowly from the bedroom, thinking her father was sleeping and someone else was in the house, but were greeted by the sight of her father lying helpless on the floor, his face sagging, his eyes and mouth wide open as if he's shouting but no sound came forth. Daddy! Daddy! She screamed as the mirror of her father's condition caused her to respond to her father as if five years ago when she last named him daddy. Everything will be ok, daddy, I will get help! Confused, she tried to find the phone and finally found it and called for an ambulance. Oh God, please save my father she called on the spiritual mirror of healing and restoration, sometimes mostly called on by desperation and when we are pleading for the mirrors view to change. While Alison is waiting for the ambulance to arrive, his mirror of the father is reflecting so many images in front of her. Death being one of the reflections. Often when a traumatic experience sweeps us off our feet, we tend to think the worst might happen but we forget that the final say is not with us but with our heavenly father as we are created in his image, he need to reflect on his image of healing, provision, restoration and faith and continue to look in his heavenly spiritual reflection of perfection. Getting back to Alison's story, the ambulance staff arrived, one them looking concerned as he tries to assist her father. They do what they can, put her father on the stretcher and leave for hospital with Alison with her father, holding his hand, saying a silent prayer.

Chapter 3:

Mirror of Patience and Faith

At the hospital, her father is rushed to the ICU. At reception, they ask her medical and insurance questions a 15 year old would not know or care about. Wait, Alison said, I will call my mother as she know these stuff. Still in shock, adrenaline fueled, she calls her mother's cell phone. Hello, a voice says on the other side. Mommy, mommy, mommy is all her mother can her. Alison? When last did I hear you call me mommy? She actually felt so needed when her daughter uttered those words but her joy would turn to concern as Alison told her what happened. A wife will show her colors when her family is in trouble and her mirror will reflect of motherly and wife affections as only a mommy can. Within a few minutes, Alison's mother was at hospital with her handbag full of information, medical insurance etc. needed for her husband to be assisted. He worked so hard all these years and he never took sick so his insurance would be happy to help, she thought. She gave the insurance details to reception who intern called the insurance company to confirm membership. Yes, I see, thank you for your time and she put the phone down. Mam, I'm sorry but they confirmed your husband cancelled his insurance 6 months ago. Alison's mom is shocked, how? I don't understand? Well we can help but you will be responsible for the hospital bill. Fine, mom replied, we will deal with the bill. Putting aside the questions relating to the insurance, she rushed to her husband's side. Where Kelvin Anderson is pleased, she asked at ICU and they showed her where he is. When she and Alison entered the room, a group of doctors surrounded her husband. Can anyone tell me what is wrong with my husband, she asked? The doctors turned around and one came to her. Mrs. Anderson, I have some news for you. Your husband has suffered a hemorrhage to the brain which have caused a lot of swelling. We have placed him in an artificial coma to help the swelling to go down and stop the bleeding. Only time will tell, prayer is needed now and faith. Are you a Christian, Mrs. Anderson, the doctor asked? Well...No, yes I have gone to church. Mrs. Anderson I will pray for you and your family the doctor said and left. Alison held her mom. Mommy whets going to happen? Time will tell baby she said. The reality was that her husband and her father could die; the reality was that he could leave them this time without saying goodbye. Daddy is not doing a sales call this time; he is not at home too tired to talk. At this time Alison and her mother would have wanted it to be the latter she is off on a sales call and not in this hospital. The mirror of Kelvin in hospital has been on both of their minds as they leave for home. There is nothing they can do by just being there. Time will tell, they were told. How sometimes we look in our daily mirrors and do not like what we see but if the mirror changes, we want what we took for granted back and therefore refuse to move forward, clinging on to the old mirror image. That night at home, none of them could sleep. Alison came in crept in bed with mommy. Mommy, I'm scared, she said. Don't be scared baby, her mom said. Your father will be well tomorrow and he will come through that door saying, where my breakfast woman? They both laughed at the thought and expectation and hoped that would come through, but will it?

Chapter 4:
The Mirror of Disappointment

The next day, both Alison and her mom woke up early, made breakfast for three and waited patiently for such was their mirrors of expectation that they believed it will come true. An hour past, two then four, then seven but no sign of daddy. Suddenly Alison screamed of frustration. If you did not leave daddy that note, he would be here today! What, her mom surprisingly replied. Her mom completely forgotten about the note. Did I kill my husband, she thought? What have I done? She fell to her knees and for the first time in years out of frustration called the Lord and said, what I have done. Isn't it amazing how the lords image comes when we are at our lowest, as if God is reflecting his presence on us, for us to turn to him? Alison, stunned by what she said, fell on his knees next to her mother and said, mommy I didn't mean to say that, please forgive me, they hugged each other as they cried without volume control, crying out their frustration and concern. When they were finished, they looked at some album pictures of them as a family. As Alison reached on the top shelve to get the remaining albums, he lost grip and the albums fell. There was a bible between the album and the bible fell open and had psalm 91 open. Look mommy, Alison said. What is that asked her mom? It's grandma's old bible. Put it away her mom said but Alison felt the need to read the psalm which she did, twice, three times. She felt an attraction to the reflection of the spiritual mirror and message within the Bible. Mommy when last did we go visit grandma? Her mom and grandma have not spoken for years after an argument over grandma wanting to force what he thought as religious beliefs on her. I don't remember, Alison, she said. Can we go visit grandma after visiting daddy please? Reluctantly she agreed. Alison had a sudden burning desire to see her grandma, not knowing the mirror the bible have prepared for her for her future if she will only look and believe. Later that day, they went to hospital with high hopes of taking daddy home. Like when she was six years old, Alison held her mommy's hand and walked to the hospital room. Another doctor was there checking his medical report. I doctor imp his wife, Mary. How is he doing? Is this your daughter? Yes she replied. Well we still hope for the best but the cancer has spread and was trying to elevate the pressure on his brain. Cancer, both mother and daughter scream out? Yes, I'm sorry they picked it up on the latest report. Also I see you have no medical insurance. The reality is that the cost could run into hundreds of thousands of dollars. If there is no recovery and you cannot afford to pay for his hospitalization, then....What doctor, Alison's mom asked. Then according to medical process, the legal spouse may opt for the life support to be switched off. There is a very slim chance of him recovering and he might be brain dead for life. I'm sorry but I had to give you all the options. Confused and angry, Alison said, mommy can we afford to pay for daddy's hospital? What can we do? Doctor, thank you for informing us but my husband will recover and we can pay the bill, in her heart, she did not know how but she kept her stance badly. Come on Alison, let's go, Bye Kelvin, Bye daddy they both said and left. Mary kept her tears from Alison but did not know for how long she could. Can we go to grandma now? Yes her mom said and they drove to grandma's house.

Chapter 5:
The Mirror of Destiny

Grandma, or granny Mabel as known to all in the community lived on her own in downing street in a huge house build in 1969 by her husband that have passed away many years ago. They stop in the front yard, Mary expecting the worst as they have not talked for years. Granny Mabel opened that door as if they never had any argument, grabbed and hugged both Alison and Mary. Oh Lord, my prayers have been answered. Come in, come in. Alison when last did I see you, let grandma give you a lollipop. Thank you, Alison said and licked it like she was a little girl. Now what bring you two here, not that imp complaining? Well, we just came to say hello and....and...And. Yes I'm listening my child grandma told her daughter as she could sense something is very wrong. Momma Kelvin is dying, he has cancer and they say he not going to make it. Tears streaming down her face as she could not help herself. She in her mature age is in her mother's mirror and a mother always knows how to reflect that image of hope and belief in their child's life. Grandma let both of them rest on her chest and as both cried, she consoled them with a bible hymn. The lord is faithful and the lord will provide. Momma what have the Lord ever done for us, how can you still believe, Mary told grandma. Well, my child, stay here as long as you like and I will show you what God can do. Mary had the mirror of unbelief that she has been looking at, even idolizing for too long. She was consumed with self-trust and her mother saw that. The mirror of unbelief need to be broken, grandmamma thought. Lord, you brought my child home for a reason helps me help her fight the good fight. Let's all go to bed, have a good night's rest and we can talk tomorrow. Saturday is a good day for catching up. Grandma chuckled and gave them both a hug. Mary I'm not going to show you where to sleep in your own house. Good night then. Goodnight they both said. Alison went straight to bed, her mind fatigued from what have happened but her mom could not sleep and she decided to go down to the basement where she had such fond memories playing as a child. I wonder if it still looks the same, she thought, going the stairs and switching on the light, she saw a brighter light then the light she just switched on and suddenly a soft voice spoke to her. Mary, see yourself as I see you. Still shielding her eyes from the light, she could not understand the words or what is going on. The bright light became dim and she could not comprehend if she was hallucinating or not but what she saw in the basement filled her with surprise. As you enter the basement, there is a big mirror, with the words Gods mirror at the top. Against the walls are all pictures of family members and prayer verses next to each picture. There were such a lot of prayers and verses that she doesn't know how her mother found time to do all this. She wanted to walk away but there was something within her that wanted her to stay to read. Well, I have nothing to lose she thought. She read all she could and fell asleep whilst reading. Was the mirror of unbelief broken? We need to understand that the mirror we carry in our daily lives is a reflection of who we are and we must be selective in our choice of mirrors as the images those mirror show is who we will be molded into through the holy spirit.

Chapter 6:
The Mirror of the Holy Spirit

The next morning as the sun rose and it was a beautiful day, Mary was woken by the rooster crowing in her mother's yard. Still trying to figure out what she experienced last night,

Rubbing her eyes and yawning like there is no tomorrow, she forgot all what she was thinking and reality of her husband jumped in her thoughts. I must get ready, I must go, she said. As she went upstairs from the basement door, she could smell freshly baked bread as she used to smell when she was little. In the kitchen the found momma and Alison busy with breakfast. Look mommy at the bread I made. Grandma showed me how. That great honey, Mary said but we need to get dressed and go see your father. First eat your breakfast, it's no use starting the day of hungry, grandma Mabel said. As they sat at the table, grandma said grace but both Alison and her mom did not close their eyes for they have not prayed as a family for long, they have forgotten the reason for being grateful before your meal. Momma? Yes

Mary, grandma said. Can you please tell me what you have done to the basement? The big mirror and the entrance and all the family pictures and prayers against the wall? Well baby, those are my wall of remembrance of the mirrors of good times in our family. The reflections of faith in those images that God have given us joy and happiness in those images and God will do it again. Those pictures you see are pictures where the family was still molded in faith, where we still believed in happiness and the prayers are for all my family as I know them, happy and blessed. Mary if you saw your pictures on the wall, those were when you were in your teens, happy, looking forward to life and loving yourself and those around you. When I pray I look at those reflections of happiness in your eyes and I'm reminded that God is real and he has not left us. Those pictures images are in my memory and seeing them while I pray gave me such hope over the years. Your daddy's pictures are a reflection of a time when we had such love for each other and we were each other best friend, before the crash which took him to the Lord. His reflection of love and those images on the wall gave me hope and as you and I have not spoken for a while, I never kept praying for you my child and God brought you back to me. But what about the mirror, Mary asked? When

I leave after prayer and look in the mirror, I'm reminded that I'm still standing and God have kept my image of hope through the storms and even though my skin is wrinkly and old, God still see me as his child, his prefect creation. Hats like the words I heard in the basement, Mary said with doubt as if she does not even believe what she said. The voice said I want you to see me as I see you. That was God, giving you hope, grandma said. Lord let your will be done, she shouted! Momma, please can we pray tonight, Mary asked? Yes that would be cool, Alison said. I will love that but let's get ready and go see Kelvin, I'm coming with, grandma said. The heavenly mirror in your life will always resurface even if you intended to bury those images. When God calls you, all that you thought have caused you so much pain in your life have been used to bring you closer to heavens calling. Mary saw Gods spiritual mirror calling her and through her, she have reflected on her daughter and the reflection will be carried over from one to another. Grandma started it through not giving up on the visions the heavenly mirror presents to all that call on God and accept the Lord Jesus as our savior.

Chapter 7:
The Mirror of Love

As they arrived at Kelvin's room, they were greeted by an empty bed. Shocked, Mary looked at Alison. Is daddy. Is daddy? Streams of tears ran down Alison's face. I can't lose my daddy now. Help me, lord, please. Grandma was standing, emotionless with the bible in her hands. A nurse came in and sadisms Anderson? Yes, Mary said, expecting the worse. Your husband is currently in MRI having some cat's cans done. The doctor will be with you shortly and she left. A sigh of relieving could be heard as the nurse left the room. Before the doctor came, the ward secretary came, Mrs. Anderson I just need you to sign this form for costs regarding your husband's hospitalization and total costs involved. Grandma looked, listened and still said nothing. Sure Mary said and signed the document. The costs did not matter to her anymore; she is starting to believe within herself that all will be well even though she does not know it yet. Then the doctor came, Mr. Anderson, your husband test results came back, there is currently no brain activity. What does that mean, doctor? Your husband is brain dead. We are keeping him alive artificially. It is your choice now as what you want to do next. Alison, hearing

Words she never thought she would hear, pain she never thought she would feel, as if her body is riddled with pain. NO! NO! Alison shouted and ran out of the room. Alison! Her mom called, but she just ran. She fell and started crying uncontrollably. Lord, please help us, she shouted out. Don't you love us anymore! If you are here, help my father please, I'm begging you! Suddenly she felt a hand on her shoulder. In shock, she replied, God is it you? No but GOD is here, the voice said. Can I help you child, a man's voice said. As she tried to look at the image, the sun reflecting in her eyes stopped her from seeing who it is. Suddenly she saw her mother. Alison are you okays mommy, where is the man? What man, her mom asked? Confused at all that have happened, she just grabbed her mother and said, I love you. Those words were what Alison's mom wanted to hear for so long. She longed for touch of love from her husband and daughter. Look at me Alison, Mary said. We are not giving up on daddy, we are not giving up. God will help us. We need to believe and all will be well. The heavenly mirror has started its reflection on mother and daughter and right there on the floor, they gave their life to Jesus and believed that a miracle will happen. When they walked into the hospital room, Kelvin was back in the room, grandma has placed the bible with a mirror reflective cover in his folded unresponsive arms. They held hands and said a prayer. Where two or more agree on Lord, you say in your word, that miracles will happen so we believe and we remind you of your word. Amen. Why the mirror bible mom, Mary asked? So when we wake up, he can see how God see him, a triumph over death, a testimony, a hope where there were none. They believed, kissed Kelvin goodbye for the night and left. That night, all three of them went into the basement, praying as they enter, looking at their daily mirrors and reflecting on God's word in prayer. They learned to fight the good fight, through focusing on the good God have done through their lives and the painful images what once were their mirrors, which they replaced with heavenly mirrors of peace and faith. They worshipped and looked at the mirror after they finished, remembering they are still standing through the storm and still smiling

Chapter 8:
The Mirror of Patience

Sunday morning they got ready for church. It feels too weird I haven't been at church for years, Mary said. Her husband, Kelvin is a non-believer and they since have believed in self-effort brings value but Mary has vivid memories of being brought up in a Christian home where God and church kept the family together, mirror of reflections she held on to in her subconscious until today. The lord will be so happy to have you back in his house, her momma said. Can I wear your earrings mommy, Alison asked. Yes, baby sure, Mary said with a smile. They left for church and as they entered the church doors, they were greeted by mirrors of smiles and acceptance, far from what Mary thought she would experience. Grannie Mabel, is this little Mary, an elderly lady asked. Yes she is, her momma said proudly. Welcome baby and this beautiful young lady. I'm Alison. Pleasure to meet you, the elderly lady said. The pastor greeted them as though he knew them forever as he knew granny Mable and her mirror have an effect on all around her. The service started and pastern was preaching after worship on faith and endurance in hardships. As the pastors preached, Alison heard what she never heard before as she has never been in a church until today. She was so taken with the word that she was staring with her mouth open. Grandma, watching her, gave her a mint and said, you hungry baby? No grandma, but her hunger for the word increased, not the physical but the spiritual.

Alison's mom had the same effect fall on her, though she were raised in church, the absence of the word have been reignited. As if a flame that were dead have resurfaced and as a furnace have taken over. Alison enjoyed it so much she started to feel so much joy, joy she never knew. Alter call came and both Alison and her mother gave their hearts to GOD with no fear, no doubt, just faith. After church, they drove home, still singing the service hymns as they felt the heavenly mirror reflecting on them. For that brief moment, Alison and Mary forgot about their storms, but the mirror of reality resurfaced when they got home and the thought of their father and husband entered their minds. At dinner time they were quiet at the table. How did you find the service, grandma asked? Fine, they both replied. Grannie Mabel knew they were being tormented by the visions of reality and decided to intervene. Look, my children, let me tell you something. The devil flashes these mirrors of trauma, illness, heartache and all he can in front of us to distract us from looking at Gods heavenly mirror of healing, restoration ,love and all that is good. Don't let him win please. It's so hard mother, Mary said. We have to go, Alison has school tomorrow. Thank you momma for everything, we love you. They left that night victors even though they felt like victims and left and momma waved them goodbye, Mabel knew their heavenly mirror will provide but not overnight. Lord please provides them with the vision of patience, she prayed softly.

Afterwards life sort off went on, Alison by school, mom at home. The day, turned into weeks and to two months, two days and still no improvement. The bills Mary received both from hospital and the mortgage started to reflect on her face, a mirror of tiredness. At school, everyone where giving Alison well wishes with her father. She kept her head up, still believing but also the mirror of doubt crept in, leaving her screaming at night, waking up from nightmares of seeing her father's grave and how she never said goodbye and how she was with her father before all happened. She stood up from bed, looked at her mirror and said, this is how GOD see me and she smiled and made a silly pose. Devil you are not going me show me sad mirrors again, be gone in Jesus name and she read from the bible given to her at church. Yes one has to stand up to your mirror if it's not Gods heavenly image meant for you. She heard a whimpering softly and it came from her mother's room. Her mother was lying in a fetal position and tears were flowing. Mommy are you ok? No baby, no I'm not. Your father is not getting better, the hospital bills are piling up and we might lose this house. We have just enough for food for his month. I called your father's workplace to find out if they could help and they told me he was fired there nine months ago. I found a few numbers in your fathers drawers that showed work next to them. I called the numbers and was told your father only works there part time so he had two jobs so he could support us and he never told us he lost his sales rep job. The two jobs he had do not have any benefits so I don't know what to do. Alison could see the pain in her mother's eyes, something she has not seen so intensely. She took her mom by the hand, lifted her and sat next to her. She held her mom and she started to say the Our Father prayer and her mommy said the prayer with. Without saying anything else, Alison gave her mom a hug and went to bed and Mary did the same.

Chapter 9:
The Mirror of Grace

At school, Alison became more withdrawn and have not practiced with her softball team since it happened. She was also do not hanging out with them at the cafeteria as her main concern is her father and mother. Although they knew her situation, she did not want to be pestered with questions relating to the father, the reality of it all were bad enough. As she sat on the steps at the school hall, her softball teammates came beeches Alison, they all said. Hey guys, she said, feeling awkward at most. Jane, the team captain said, Alison, do you mind coming to the clubhouse. There is something I want to discuss with you. All right then Alison said. Anything to avoid any questions. Maybe they are kicking me off the team she thought. At this point, she could not care and as she entered the clubhouse door, she was surprised by almost the whole school cheering and giving her hugs, even the bradmin twins that she thought hated her. Shocked, Alison asked, what is happening? Her teacher came forth, gave her a hug and said, Alison we just want to show you how much we care about you. We know that is a tough time for you and we want you to know we love you. Principle Stevens stepped in and said, Alison we have secretly been doing fundraisers and have raised a total of 95000 dollars in total, mostly donations from business people for you and your mother to help with costs. Alison just looked at all of them, looked at their smiles, their affection and thought, there must be a God. With tears in her eyes she accepted the check and thanked all that have helped. She felt so full of joy and knew that this was God working. After school she rushed home, stormed through the door and found her mother crying. Mommy I have good news. What is it Alison? I'm just tired of everything, Mary said. Mommy the school has raised 95000 dollars for us. Isn't God great? What? Alison say again? 95000 dollars mommy. Mary could not believe what she was hearing as she has been counting the total of all bills that have been piling up and it amounted to 80000 dollars. Mary just fell down and knelt on the floor, lifting her hands high and praising God for hearing her prayers. Alison held her mom in joy. Grace has been reflected on them as God knew when they needed when they needed it. Later that night Mary called her mother to share the great news. Ah,

God is great, Grandma Mabel rejoiced. See my child that was grace. What is grace, Mary asked? Grace is when we are given a second chance even though you did not deserve it. It is when God steps in when you no longer can. Momma, what can I do to live how God want us to live? Well Mary, when you go shopping and you see that perfect dress you desire in the shop window. Do you need the dress or want it? It's the same with the mirrors within our daily lives. The devil uses a mirror to make us mimic sin in disguise. He will let people see riches in ones mirror but not reflect the way he obtained those riches. He will make the mirror too tempting but he will not show you how the mirrors image came about. When looking at such worldly mirrors which is not according to Gods will, we must ask ourselves; do we need it or want it? Every day we see the devils mirror being shone at us, trying to make us mimic the mirror they reflect of anger, hate, violence and all that is not Gods will for us. Do not mimic those actions instead do the opposite as this cause those mirrors of unbelief to be break. We need to be steadfast in our faith, my child. Thank you momma, I got to go now. I'll be praying for you Mary, send my love to Alison. Will do, bye. As Mary dropped the phone, she was thinking how she can get closer to God. Then she thought, well momma is my mirror, il reflect on what she taught me. Mary started the put pictures of her family of joyful times on the walls, she started to read scriptures from the bible and she took an old big mirror from the bedroom and placed it nearby. She started to read the bible and became almost as if she felt as one with what she read from the bible as the spiritual mirror reflected on her. She did not know it but Alison was also reading her bible and putting prayer versus with heart stickers against her bedroom wall. Such is the effect of the spiritual mirror in our daily lives that the Holy Spirit will let all fall into place. Mary called Alison down stairs. Alison looked around seeing all her mom done and said, mommy I also did the same in my room, gosh so cool. Yes cool indeed, Mary smiled. Let's pray, as Mary started, Devil, your mirror have been broken in this house! You have no place to shed your sin reflections anymore. We are Gods children and we love Jesus. We rebuke you in the name of Jesus and we are sick of you trying to ruin our lives. This house is Under Gods rule and you have been evicted. Thank you God for healing my husband and healing our family, in Jesus name we pray, Amen! Alison, do you want to pray, Mary asked. Yes mommy but you said all I wanted to say so I'll just agree, Amen! Agreed then, give me a high five, Alison. Cool mommy so what do we do now? Now we stay in faith and believe and resist the devil and he will flee. Mommy, I have a softball match on Thursday, will you come? Sure baby, I will be there, promise. Thank you mommy, Alison was so glad. Let's go, it's almost visiting time so I can tell daddy and read him a verse from the bible. Let's go then, Mary said.

Chapter 10:
The Mirror of Faith

At hospital, the change of atmosphere could be felt within the hospital room. There was an atmosphere of hope. As they came there, Kelvin still had the bible under his lifeless folded arms but there where an expectation of belief. Daddy, guess what, mommy will be at my softball game on Thursday and I also want you to be there. You don't have to give me an answer just yet. I have a verse from the bible I want to read to you about Lazarus and how Jesus raised him from the dead after four days. As Alison read to her father, Mary just watched with amazement and joy. Her family was together and for the first time in years, they were in the same room and communicating. Even though the circumstances are not as desired, it is just so wonderful what God have done for them and whatever happens she will cherish this moment forever. Even it this time of storms, she got to know her mother again and her daughter and their bond are stronger than ever, something she never thought would be possible. She remembered the song amazing grace and started singing it softly as Alison, glanced at her and smiling and continued to read to her father. Once Alison finished reading, they both kissed their father and husband on the forehead and was about to leave when the doctor came in. Mrs. Anderson, I was just about to call you. The MRI results for today came in and it looks like there is a slight brain activity taken place. Now it does not guarantee anything but there is life within your husband's brain though how small. We always inform the spouse in a situation as such that the patient might regain some activity but they might be in a vegetative state. Thank you doctor for the news, this is the best news ever. Before I was told that to switch off the life support was the only option, now there is life and as you say the activity is small, I believe and with my daughter and mommas faith, even as small as a mustard seed that all is well. Well...goodbye then, doctor said. Goodbye doctor. Faith is like a mirror, your mirror is God, your reflection is of God and your actions mimicked of the mirror of the word within the bible. Mary has entered a realm to understanding how God works within our hearts as your hearts are like a mirror and it reflects what it attracts and if you allow your heart to image the word of God then the supernatural will manifest and will be shown through the mirror within. As it says in the bible, James 1:22-25 which reads, but be doers of the word, and not hearers only, deceiving yourselves. For if anyone is a hearer of the word and not a doer, he is like a man who looks intently at his natural face in the mirror. For the looks at himself and goes away and at once forgets what he was like. But the one who looks into the perfect law, the law of liberty, and perseveres, being no hearer who forgets but a doer who acts, he will be blessed in his doing. 1 Corinthians 13:12 reads, For now, we see in a mirror dimly, but then face to face. Now I know in part, then I shall know fully, even as I have been fully known. The next day, Alison went to school and Mary was busy washing dishes when she heard the bell rang. Just a minute, she said while drying her hands. She opened the door and it was her next door neighbor, Gladys. Mary was shocked as she was an introvert and she seldomely came out of her house but they always respected each other. Hi Gladys, how are you? I'm fine Mary and how are you? I heard Kelvin was in hospital and I brought you some bread rolls I made. That's very kind of you. How is your husband? Well Clive have been diagnosed with prostate cancer and he have been admitted earlier this week but we are keeping the faith for a full recovery. I'm so sorry to hear that, Gladys. I will pray for you and if you want you can join me for prayer tonight here at our house and if you are free, I would like to invite you for dinner. Gladys went silent all of a sudden. It's have been a while since she has had any social activity, having dinner outside her house was something she tried to avoid but she felt the mirror of sincerity shining from Mary and she said with tears in her eyes, that would be wonderful. What time should I be here? What can I bring? Just bring yourself Gladys, Mary said with a smile. Good, see you later then Mary. I look forward to it Gladys and she left.

Chapter 11:
The Mirror of Two or More in Agreement

Mary was busy getting ready for night time prayer and dinner. Alison came home and greeted her mommy. How was your day Alison? It was great mommy. I added the bible study course to my study flow. That's wonderful, oh we have a guest tonight, Gladys from next door will join us for dinner and prayer. Aunt Gladys that never leave her house? Yes honey, she is having a hard time now and we need to encourage each other. Do your homework please and get ready for dinner afterwards. Yes mommy. Alison turn around to leave and suddenly turned around looking at her mom without saying anything. What's wrong Alison? Nothing, I'm just glad when I look at how things are changing. I am too Hun, go now and she made like she was going to hit Alison with the washcloth. Love you mom, Alison's said to her mom and she left, leaving Mary with a warm heart. Just as Mary was about to resume her duties the phone rang. Hello, Hi Mary, it's Gladys. May I ask if I may invite a few people with for prayer and don't worry, they will bring their own dinner. Sure Gladys but there is enough food to share. Don't worry Mary all is well. See you later, bye. Bye, Mary said. She was surprised at the request of Gladys. I never knew this would even happen but your will Lord, your will and she resumed getting ready. It's probably just this one extra person? Maybe they won't even come, Mary thought. At five past six, the doorbell rang. Alison came in to open the door. No baby, I will open in and Mary walked to the door. As she opened the door, she was hit by surprise as the whole neighborhood, at least most women were on her doorstep, each carrying a pot and the smells coming from there were tremendous. Still surprised but keeping her curiosity, she invited all in with smile. Please put your pots on the dining room table and have a seat. I must say I am pleasantly surprised to see all of you here. Mrs. Connoly looked at Mary and said, Mary please forgive us for entering your home in the crowd we see before you. We are here to give you support in your time of need but we were also curious as when we saw Gladys leave her house to go to your house and we heard about the prayer session and we want to be part of it. Well, I'm honored to have you here. Alison please helps with serving our neighbors their choice of tea or coffee and afterwards we can have dinner. Please all, make yourself at home. They later enjoyed their dinner with all the different favors and tastes from each individual at the table and they laughed at Aunt May's tales of the old days when she used to be a cattle farmer and Mr. Jones army tales and even Mrs. Paine, who always complained and never laughed, could not help herself from expressing her joy. Later they engaged in prayer, individually and as in a group. The worshipped and praised and all brought their requests forth to God and Mr. Jones started playing the piano as they sang hymns and went into to mirror of faith. Everyone thanked Mary for the night and did not want the night to end. They decided to make this a monthly occasion to feed their spirits and to fellowship with each other. Mary stood up and said, I thank you all for being here; I needed this more than you all know. Thank you for your mirror of faith that you brought in our house and the images reflected tonight I shall never forget. No, we have to thank you, Mrs. Paine said but may I ask why is there a mirror and all the photos and prayers against your wall? It is my remembrance of what God have done through my life, my prayers that were answered and when looking at the mirror I'm reminded that I'm still standing through the storm that when I see me, I see God as we were created in his perfect image. We all are created in the image of God and our reflections each day is a mirror to others who seek the heavenly mirror in their lives, who have not looked in the mirror for years for fear what they might see. Every day we walk past mirrors, mirrors that smile at us, mirrors that frown and us, that make us feel bad and today I were in the company of mirror that made me full of Joy and this is how God want us to see ourselves. The devil uses human mirrors to change our mirror. So if you meet someone today, tomorrow or whenever that frown at you, shout at you, make you feel bad about yourself, smile at the mirror and in time that mirror will smile back at you and the devils mirror will be broken. Amen, everyone shouted! They hugged each other and left. Mary and Alison went to bed that night with a peace that they have not had in a while.

Chapter 12:
Faith Like a Mirror

How are our faith defined? How do we understand what faith means? What does a mirror have to do with faith? Well, I also asked these questions and had to observe myself, my daily reactions towards the daily problems that we face and how we deal with it. Have you noticed how whenever you pray for faith, the storm comes immediately afterwards. I believe faith is the Devils worst enemy and he will try his last best to throw you from your faith by flashing mirrors of unbelief, doubt and everything he can at you. Notice that when you gave your heart to Jesus, almost immediately after thing looked like they were worse. People looking at you with frowns and anger which you don't even know. Things happened that are trying to change your emotional state. That is the devil hiding behind that human mirror of anger and all things opposite to Gods will for you, wanting you to copy those actions and to take away your faith. Have you also noticed that giving into these mirrors and copying these actions will drain you, make you depressed and keep you from your initial focus. One time I gave a car guard money who looked after my car at the mall. He praised and thanked me so much and I felt all the glory should go to God not me so I said he must thank God for what he has given him. The guard told me said, yes but I don't see God now but I see you. We are representing God on this earth and how people see us is reflective of God they see in our mirror. Corinthians 3:18 reads, But we all, with unveiled face, beholding as in a mirror the glory of the Lord, are being transformed into the same image from glory to glory, just as from the Lord, the spirit. Hebrews 11; 1 reads, Now faith is the assurance of things hoped for, the conviction of things not seen. What are you hoping to see in your mirror or others to see in your mirror today? See yourself as God sees you, courageous, unstoppable and a child of the most high.

Here are some inspirational Bible verses as you reflect on your daily mirror of faith.

Jeremiah 29:11 reads, For I know the plans I have for you, declares the Lord, plans to prosper you and not to harm you, plans to give you hope and a future.

Psalm 27:4 reads One thing I ask from the lord,

this only do I seek, that I may dwell in the house of the Lord all the days of my life, to gaze on the beauty of the Lord and seek him in his temple.

Psalm 34; 8 reads, Taste and see the lord is good, blessed is the one who takes refuge in him

Isaiah 40:28:-31 reads, Do you not know, Have you not hear? The Lord is the everlasting God, the Creator of the ends of the earth. He will not grow tired or weary, and his understanding no one can fathom. He gives strength to the weary and increases the power to the weak. Even youths grow tired and weary, and young men stumble and fall, but those who hope in the lord will renew their strength. They will soar on the wings on eagles, they will run and not grow weary, and they will walk and not be faint.

2 Corinthians 4:16-18

Therefore, we do not lose heart. Though outwardly we are wasting away, yet inwardly we are being renewed day by day. For our light and momentary troubles are achieving for us an eternal glory that far outweighs them all. So we fix our eyes not on what is seen, but on what is unseen, since what is seen is temporary, but what is unseen is eternal.

Corinthians 16: 13

Be on your guard, stand firm in faith, be courageous, be strong

James 1: 2-4

Consider it pure joy, my brothers and sisters, whenever you face trials of many kinds, because you know that the testing of your faith produces perseverance. Let perseverance finish its work so that you may be mature and complete, not lacking anything.

Chapter 13:
The Mirror of Joy Within the Test

It's been four months since Kelvin was admitted to hospital. There was still no improvement other than the weak brain activity and the hospital bill which were paid, gaining another few thousand but Mary and Alison remained in faith, they had nothing to lose and had placed their trust in the lord. The prayer group has also increased, so much that they are having prayer meetings in the basement which is much bigger. Mary started to notice that Gladys had not attended the last prayer session. She does not have a cell phone and her home telephone number is just ringing so Mary went to her house to see how Gladys is. Mary rang the doorbell. Who is it, sounded beyond the door. It's me, Mary. Come in Mary and she opened the door. Gladys sat in the living room with her photo album in her hands. I loved him so much, I...I don't know why this happened. Gladys, what happened, Mary asked. The Lord took Clive away from me Mary. Why, when I give my life to him? Why when I asked him to take his pain and suffering away? Why? Gladys broke down in tears as Mary sat next to her as Gladys wept on her shoulder. The pain of mourning could be felt like a cold chill throughout the house which was once a home. Gladys had no family; she was an orphan and only had Clive. They were married for forty-five years, a lifetime of togetherness and now it's gone. Mary did not say anything, she let Gladys cry her heart out as she could relate to her pain, though her husband still lived, sometimes she wondered will he ever be here again? Now she is face to face with a loss and wonder if she will also face the same fate. The mirror of doubt crept in, shining an image of death. Mary thought of her pledge to God and that she has faith that all will be well. She looked at Gladys and said, I don't know why this happened but I know God have taken Clive's pain and suffering away and given him eternal life. A heavenly mirror he sees and experiences a life with no pain and no suffering and one day, we all will join Clive in heaven. Glady heard her friend and realized just what she said was true and his pain and suffering are gone and even though it is not how she wanted it to be, he is free and free indeed. Thank you Mary, I realize that my Clive is well now, all is well and soon I will see him. Can we pray Mary, please? Yes we can Gladys, Mary replied and they prayed our father who art in heaven and both received a feeling of peace. Now I can go on Mary, the Lord is good and I ask forgiveness for doubting him. They did not realize it yet but they both broke the mirror of doubt the enemy wanted them to look at. Suddenly Mary's phone rang. It was the hospital. Mrs. Anderson, this is Doctor Stevens, Kelvins doctor. Would it be possible if you can come to hospital please, I have something to tell you. Oh yes DR., I'll be right there and she ended the call. Gladys I'm so sorry to have to leave you now but I just received a call from the hospital. No need to explain Mary, I'll be just fine. Tell Kelvin I said Hi, Gladys said in faith, Yes I will, take care bye. Bye Mary, Gladys said. While Mary is on the way home to get the car and get Alison, a lot of questions to the call from hospital arise. Every time doubt crept in, Mary keep saying, Devil, your mirror won't work on me. Doubt leaves my mind, in Jesus name. She came home, Alison was busy studying. Baby we must go now, hospital called. Is it daddy? Is he awake? Alison had such and excitement in her voice. I don't know, Mary said and they left for hospital.

Chapter 14:
The Mirror of Endurance

Alison and Mary arrived at the hospital and started to run towards the hallway as though they were running to get a trophy, with joy in their eyes and an expectation of good news as they ran and came out of breath in the hospital room to find two doctors and three nurses standing over Kelvin. Hi, I'm Mrs. Anderson, I received a call...?Yes Mrs. Anderson, one of the doctors said, your husband is currently in a comatose state as you know but he had suffered two heart attacks today. We managed to revive him, but this heart has taken a lot of pressure from these attacks and his heart rate is slow, below normal. We don't know what will happen next and don't know if we will be so lucky next time to have his heart beat again. From my experience, this in an indication of heart failure. I'm sorry Mrs. Anderson, we have tried all we could. Alison, not being able to handle all that were just mentioned, started to scream in a fit of range, anger and sadness and holding her head while sitting in the corner of the room. She was screaming, daddy, daddy, daddy all the time and was in another state. Mary looked at the whole situation and remembered her mother's words, she remembered Gladys and her pain and she remembered her prayer group. She remembered her pictures against the wall. She remembered the mirror as she looked at it and the smile she gave as she viewed herself. She looked at her daughter, Alison as she calmed a bit from it all just sitting quietly in the corner with her head hanging. She remembered all the mirrors which she had to endure and the ones she triumphed over and realized she is and overcomer and a victor, not a victim. She knew God had more in store for her and her family and she knew what she had to do. She looked at the switch which was connected to the life support which kept her husband alive. She reached out to the switch and as she stretches her hand, all in the room are looking at her, the doctors and nurses and Alison with a look of fear and as if time stood still, all were silent. Can me and my daughter have some privacy please, Mary asked? Yes, we understand, looking at each other and a few clearing their throats, they left immediately. Alison was still sitting in the corner, looking at her mother, asking the obvious question without words as she waited for an answer. Alison, get up please and come over here. Alison walked as though she was a tightrope walker, slowly, carefully as though the end of the line could mean life or death. Mommy, what you are going to do, Alison asked sounding scared. I'm going to do something I should have done a long while ago. This has gone on too long. I should have taken action and done what is needed. Alison as confused and scared as could do not want to outer the answer she thought will come from her mother's mouth even though she had an idea what it could be. She knew what the whole ordeal have done to her mother and she did not want another parent in a lifeless state. She did not know which thought were worse. As if she were in a bad dream where she had to choose but her decision would mean heartache whatever the answer and there is no winner. She loved her mommy and daddy and wished she could turn back the hands of time but she saw the look of desperation in her mother's eyes as they looked at each other. Mary one again stretched her hand forward, as in slow-motion, the decision was based on the heart and the hands direction as to what the outcome will be. Suddenly, you could hear a pin drop in the room and Alison stood, looking at her mom with wide open eyes as her mother looked at her and said nothing as though in a trance.

Chapter 15
The Mirror of the Supernatural

Still looking at each other, mother and daughter were awaken from their expressionless state by the sound of Mary's phone ringing. Hello, Mary answered. Hi Mary, it's visiting time at the hospital; can we come to see Kelvin? Yes sure she said and ended the call. Mary had stretched her hand towards the life support switch and in thought prayed that there will be a miracle to stop the artificial support of her husband and for him to support his own body and all the organs in his body and his brain to be revived supernaturally. She went into a trance like state and can only remember a bright light obstructing her view and a voice saying, Mary all is well, all is well. She was still in shock over what she saw and her daughter was as confused as ever. What happened mommy? I believe you father is well, Mary said. Then the room door opened and the neighborhood prayer group entered including Gladys which have brought her bible with and a box of chocolates for Kelvin. For when Kelvin woke up, she smiled. They made a circle around Kelvin's bed and started to pray in faith, worshipping, confessing the Lords power. As they prayed, one could feel the warmth in the room as their prayers were emitted through the believing group. Gladys ended the prayers and said, Lord, Please hear our prayers and breath new live in Kelvin. Clive had a full life Lord; you spared him till 78. Kelvin is still young and has a whole life ahead of him. Please God almighty, let your heavenly mirror shine in this hospital room. Let your angels sing praises as we worship you. We ask in Jesus name, Amen. All in the room shouted amen. There was an atmosphere of healing proportions. Thank you, everyone, for your prayers Mary said. We trust, we believe and we have faith and let the good Lord work. Later they all left, leaving Alison and Mary also to get ready to go home. Mommy everything will be fine, won't it? Yes, Alison, it will. Now let go home and have a good night's rest. They looked at Kelvin who still had the bible on his chest with his hand folded over it. Let's go, Mary said and they greeted Kelvin and were halfway out the room when suddenly the heart monitor connected to Kelvin made a strange sound as if an ongoing siren. Doctors and nurses came rushing in, Mary and Alison standing in shock not knowing what is happening. One nurse asked, Mrs. Anderson, can you two please wait for us outside? Yes we will be just outside this door. Through the frosty glass of the top part of the door, Mary and Alison could vaguely see what they were doing. They saw them over Kelvin performing CPR and after a while hear, clear and they placing something on his chest and saw his body bounce up and then went down again. Mary knew what is was but Alison did not know. What are they doing mommy? They are trying to help daddy, baby she said. Twenty minutes that felt like hours passed and they were still busy with Kelvin. There was a mirror just opposite the door where Kelvin were and as Mary turned around to give her eyes a rest from looking through the frosty glass, the reflection in the room looked like the whole room was on fire through the mirror. She looked back at the door and back into the mirror and the image was gone. Maybe I'm just tired, Mary though, rubbing her temples to elevate a mild headache she have. After forty minutes, the doctors and nursing staff came out. Mary and Alison looked at them as if they wanted to shake the answer out of them. The suspense was driving them through the wall. Kelvin's doctor walked towards Mary and Alison, took his glasses off and pressed this thumb and index finger on his eyelids and looked at them. In what felt like forever, the doctor spoke. I'm sorry, we did all we could. Those seven words felt like a dagger through their hearts as no one have spoken those words in a positive sentence. Kelvin's heart was just too weak and we tried all methods to revive him but all failed. We are sorry for your loss. Doctor spoke to the nurse and the filled in the death certificate saying, time of death, eleven thirty and he left. Alison and Mary cannot speak. Their tears speak of a battle that they cannot believe is over and ended the way it did. A story that was not supposed to end like this. Alison went inside the room, seeing the same image they have seen for months but there is no breath, no life in this picture, a body which has no spirit, a face without no emotions, staring ahead but looking nowhere. Sleeping for months but now it is eternal. Alison, sat next to her father and fell with her head on his chest, weeping uncontrollably. Daddy wake up please, she cried, daddy please listen to me. I need you, mommy needs you, and we love you. God loves you and I believe your time is not at the end on earth. I want you to watch my next softball game; I'm becoming good at it. I want you to walk me down the aisle one day when I get married. I want you to go on that vacation you and mommy used to talk about. God, I know my father is in heaven but please if it's you will, please bring my daddy home, bring my daddy home. Alison, we need to go, Mary said. They will take daddy away soon. Say your goodbyes. Mary has not seen any hope for any expectations at this point. She thanked God for the time they had with Kelvin and they will see him in heaven soon. No, no mommy this is not how it's supposed to end. Daddy looked at me as she faced her father, open your eyes. Mary could not take the hurt that she and her daughter had to endure and tried to pull Alison gently away from her father. We need to go now, Alison. She took the bible that fell on the floor when they tried to revive her dad and placed in on his chest and folded his arms over, holding the bible and kissed her father. Mary placed her arms around her daughter, almost trying to squeeze out the hurt she felt, holding her tight as only a mother could, they turned off the light and walked slowly out. The distance from the bed to the hospital room door felt like forever as they could not walk with speed they came in with when they received the call before to come to the hospital. They stood outside the open door of the dark room where Kelvin is laying, not saying a word. This would there last to see him before the funeral, something they would not want to think of. Suddenly they heard a sound of something that had fallen in the room, a sound of something with a low echo, not a heavy object. It's maybe one of the instruments they used on your father that fell, Mary said and she walked on, but in Alison's spirit she wanted to make sure. Mommy can I please just look at daddy for one more time. Mary feeling drained, just nodded and Alison turned on the light and were shocked to see the bible that were on her father chest that she folded his hands over have fallen to the ground and her father's arms were hanging off the bed on each side. Remember Alison, your father's body have no life so his arms could not hold the bible as when he was alive. It has been 45 minutes since Kelvin's death and that would be the most logical reason to justify what happened. Alison went to pick up his bible which was just underneath her father's arm hanging off the bed. As she bent down to pick up the bible, she nearly jumped on the bed in shock as she felt a hand stroking her hair as she picked up the bible. Scared with big eyes, Alison said, Daddy and she heard her father gasping for air and suddenly looking at her with open eyes. Both Alison and Mary looked at each other, is it a ghost and for that split second they almost wanted to run out but Kelvin spoke softly with his dry lips and spoke with a raspy voice, Can I have a glass of water please? Both

Mary and Alison ran out, forgetting about that was asked and ran to the nearest doctor and it was Kelvin's doctor. Doctor, doctor please come have a look, Kelvin! Yes, doctor said, looking confused. Kelvin is alive. Impossible doctor said but still his curiosity carried him towards and in the hospital room and behold Kelvin is awake. Both Mary and Alison could not say a word further and both smothered him, laying on him. Water, water, they heard underneath them in a parched, muffled voice. OH sorry, they screamed with joy and they both ran, almost falling over their feet trying to get the water. Alison came back first with the water and gave it to her father who took late sips and put the glass down. The doctors, nursing staff, Alison and Mary all looked at him with amazement. This is the man what were declared dead about fifty minutes ago and now he is sitting upright in bed, with life streaming through his veins and breath flowing from his mouth and nostrils. Kelvin's doctor walked to him and said, Mr. Anderson, we need to conduct further tests to determine what happened and how.....we need to get some medical reason for this. In my twenty years of practice, I have never experience something like this. The nursing staff and other doctor all agreed this is something not natural and that there must be reason.

How, they all asked each other, seeking medical input and theory. Alison with a wide smile looked at them and said, this is Gods supernatural healing that took place, just so God revived Lazarus from the dead after four days, so our Lord has raised my daddy from the dead after forty-five minutes. His heavenly mirror has shown on our family and he gave my father a second chance to be a father again and a husband through grace. Amen, Mary shouted! Most doctors of different ethnical and religious backgrounds, looked at each other, wrote on their notepads and walked out. One of the nurses that helped during Kelvin's heart attack came to them and said, All glory to God, I have seen the miracle of our Lord Jesus and if you don't mind, may I use what happened here as a testimony at church on Sunday? Yes, spread the good news, Mary said. Thank you, the nurse said smiling and left. Mary asked Kelvin how he feels as Alison were sitting next her daddy, holding his hand and just looking at him as if scared that if she will look away, the reality would be a dream. I feel great Mary, Kelvin said, I have such vivid visions of being in a place with shiny, gold like floors, brightness around me, a hand holding my hand as we walked though I could not see the face. A sound of trumpets and singing but the visions were too hazy for me to see and a total peace feeling. Then suddenly I opened my eyes and I see you and Alison. What happened? Why are the doctors not believing my current condition? Because you were dead for forty-five minutes and God brought you back to us daddy Alison said. Dead? Me? How long was I in hospital? Too long Hun, Mary said and Kelvin said, you know what I want to do now is to look in the mirror and see my face, I probably grew a stubby beard, laughed Kelvin. Alison took the mirror imaged bible that once laid on his chest and were held by his lifeless arms and gave it to him, here you go, daddy. A bible which a mirror image? Why?, as he looked at his reflection through the image. So you can see yourself as God sees you Kelvin, Mary says. The images you describe while dead in the natural were images of heaven and God leading you through your storm and giving you a second chance at life, as the angels rejoice. That is what I believe. Me too, Alison shouted. Me three, Kelvin said. There have got to be a God if I have been revived from death to be with my family once again. I want to give my heart to God, how do I do it? They held hands and prayed, Kelvin confessed his sins and gave his life to Lord Jesus that night. The mirrors of heaven was too majestic to deny, though they do not see, yet they believe but we all need a spiritual mirrors image to revive our faith and to see ourselves as our good Lord sees us.

Also Available By Elrich Martin